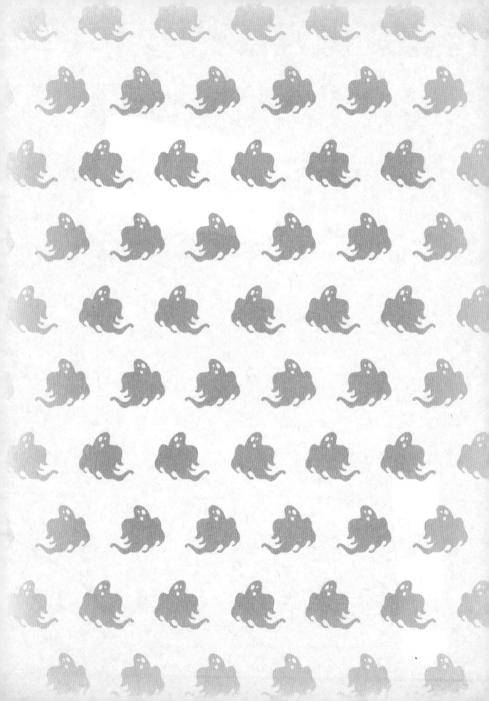

DESMOND COLE
GHOST PATROL

GHOSTS DON'T RIDE BIKES, DO THEY?

by Andres Miedoso
illustrated by Victor Rivas

LITTLE SIMON

New York   London   Toronto   Sydney   New Delhi

LITTLE SIMON

An imprint of
Simon & Schuster Children's Publishing Division
1230 Avenue of the Americas, New York, New York 10020
First Little Simon paperback edition December 2017
Copyright © 2017 by Simon & Schuster, Inc.
Also available in a Little Simon hardcover edition.
All rights reserved, including the right of reproduction
in whole or in part in any form.
LITTLE SIMON is a registered trademark of Simon & Schuster, Inc.,
and associated colophon is a trademark of Simon & Schuster, Inc.
For information about special discounts for bulk purchases, please contact
Simon & Schuster Special Sales at 1-866-506-1949 or
business@simonandschuster.com.
The Simon & Schuster Speakers Bureau can bring authors to your
live event. For more information or to book an event contact the
Simon & Schuster Speakers Bureau at 1-866-248-3049
or visit our website at www.simonspeakers.com.
Designed by Steve Scott
Manufactured in the United States of America 1117 MTN
2 4 6 8 10 9 7 5 3 1
This book has been cataloged with the Library of Congress.
ISBN 978-1-5344-1041-1 (paperback)
ISBN 978-1-5344-1042-8 (hardcover)
ISBN 978-1-5344-1043-5 (eBook)

CONTENTS

CHAPTER ONE

THRILLS AND SPILLS

Let's talk about the thrills and spills of riding a bike. Is there anything more thrilling than racing down the street with the wind in your face? Even the spills are cool. Trying to do a trick and falling off your bike, or coming home with a brand-new hole

in your jeans—it's the best! Thrills and spills. You can't have one without the other. And I wouldn't want it any other way.

The thing is, nobody ever talks about the *chills* of riding a bike. At least not until I moved to Kersville. This town is made of chills!

My bike is the coolest thing in the world. It's black with red rims. The handlebars have a compass on one side, a light in the middle, and a horn on the other side. Not a bell. A horn!

What I love about my bike is that it's not shiny and new. This bike has been through a lot of spills. There are scratches on the paint and dents to prove it. The seat even has a piece of black electrical tape from when I crashed trying to ride backward— bad idea.

The thing is, even though my bike isn't perfect, it's all mine. It's moved to every new house we've moved to, and it feels the same no matter where I live. It's basically been my best friend.

I have a real friend now. His name is Desmond Cole. He never cared about bikes before. Why?

Well, do you see that bike over there—the one with the compass, the light, and the horn? The one with the scratch on the frame and

the electrical tape on the seat? The one that's riding through the forest without anyone on it?

Yep, that's my bike.

Why is the bike riding by itself?

Well, that's a strange story.

CHAPTER TWO

GHOST SECRETS

Last week I introduced Desmond to my most prized possession in the whole world: my bike.

I opened the garage, and my bike was right there in its own spot. The sun streamed into the garage, and the light made my bike glow.

"What do you think?" I asked.

"A bike?" Desmond said flatly. "I guess it's cool."

"It's cooler than cool," I said. "Want to go riding?"

"I don't do bikes," Desmond said.

I was shocked. "Why not?"

"Because I like ghosts," he said.
What do ghosts have to do with bikes? I wondered.

Desmond must have been reading my mind. "Ghosts don't ride bikes," he said, like it was something everybody in the world already knew.

That was when Zax floated through the wall. He's a ghost, so it's not as weird as it sounds. "Andres, I need a ratchet from the toolbox."

"Wait, Zax," I said. "Let me ask you a question. Is it true that ghosts don't ride bikes?"

"Of course ghosts don't ride bikes," Zax said. Then he let out a hearty laugh that was almost as loud as his burps.

"Why not?" I asked.

"Birds don't ride bikes, do they?" Zax replied.

"Um, no," I said.

Desmond nodded. "See what I mean, Andres?"

To be honest, I was still confused.

Zax looked up from the toolbox. "Why would ghosts ride bikes when we can float everywhere?"

"Um, because riding a bike is awesome!" I said. "Speaking of awesome, I hear the Kersville Bike Park has a crazy racetrack!"

Desmond shrugged. "There won't be any ghosts there, so count me out. Have fun, and I'll see you later."

He waved good-bye and went next door into his own garage. That's where he had his Ghost Patrol office. I guess Desmond liked ghosts as much as I liked my bike.

"Found it!" Zax exclaimed, holding up the ratchet. He closed the toolbox and floated straight toward the wall. He almost made it through, but then I heard a loud **CLANG**. The ratchet dropped and smacked against the floor.

"Oh yeah," Zax said. He floated into the garage. "I keep forgetting not everything can go through walls. Can you carry this for me?"

"Okay." I kicked off my gear and took the tool. "What are you doing with this, anyway?"

Zax smiled. "It's a secret."

A secret? Something told me I wasn't going to like ghost secrets. But I put it out of my mind. I had  better things to do. I had a bike park to check out!

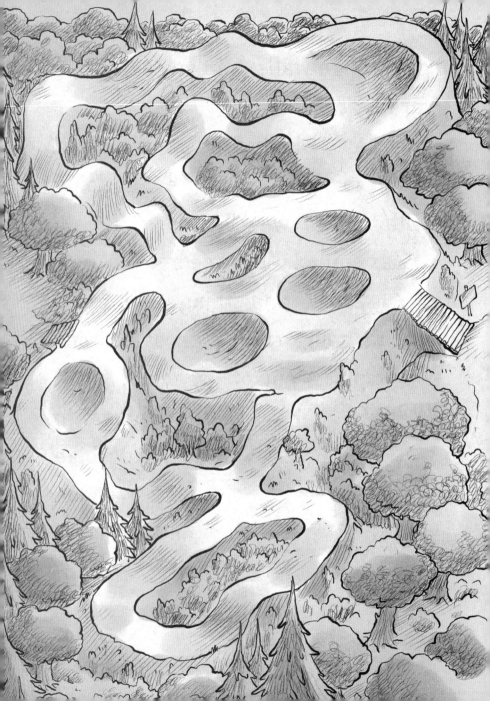

CHAPTER THREE

THE KICKER

When my parents decided to move to Kersville, they told me the town had a bike park close to our new house. That made moving here a lot easier.

The park turned out to be awesome. It had a huge dirt racetrack with way too many jumps to count.

I was prepared, though. I was wearing my helmet, kneepads, elbow pads, *and* bike gloves.

HELMET

ELBOW PADS

BIKE GLOVES

KNEEPADS

I rode over to the start of the track and waited behind a group of other kids.

"Hey, you're new here," said the boy in front of me. He pointed to the end of the track. "Whatever you do, don't ride that last jump. It's called the Kicker. Nobody ever lands it."

"Nobody?" I gulped.

"Watch and learn," he said.

A rider sped around the last turn toward the Kicker. Suddenly, her front tire lifted up into a wheelie and the girl fell off her bike. But her bike kept going! It flew up the ramp and crash-landed on the other side.

The girl got up and brushed herself off.

"The Kicker strikes again," the boy told me.

While I waited my turn, one rider after another wiped out on the Kicker. It was weird. I mean, everybody fell! Sometimes they fell to the left. Sometimes they fell to the right. One kid ended up doing a backflip into the dirt. Each time, the bike still took the jump and crashed.

I was nervous. I was a good bike rider, but I had never tried anything like the Kicker before.

Finally, it was my turn. I pedaled down the first hill fast. The track

felt good as I whipped around the first turn. I hit the first jump, held on tight, and launched into the air. It was amazing!

I landed jump after jump, and pretty soon the other kids started cheering. *For me!*

Until I came to the Kicker. At first, everything was normal. Then I felt a wave of electricity sizzle through my body. My bike started to wobble. I gripped my handlebars as the bike jerked from side to side.

Next, my pedals began to speed up

and slow down. It felt like the gears were shifting on their own!

Still, I kept my bike under control and zoomed up the Kicker. I couldn't believe it. I was going to ace the track. All I had to do was land the jump.

I flew into the air, and, man, it was exciting! I was going to do it. I was going to—

SCREECH!

My bike froze in midair. I mean, it just stopped.

Unfortunately I kept on going, right over my handlebars into a mud puddle.

My bike crashed down a second later.

I had no idea what was going on, but I knew one thing for sure. The Kicker lived up to its name.

CHAPTER FOUR

CHEDDAR CHEESE FISH FRIES

Desmond came by my house that night, and he looked really scared.

"Please help me, Andres," he said. "There is a cooking experiment at my house tonight."

"What's a cooking experiment?" I asked.

Desmond shivered. "That's when my parents use all of our leftovers to make a new meal. They are making cheddar cheese fish fries with a marshmallow dipping sauce."

My family was just having home-made chicken nuggets, corn on the cob, and salad for dinner. All of a sudden it totally sounded like the best dinner in the world.

I could see that Desmond was in trouble. I invited him inside, and we walked to the kitchen. "Mom, can Desmond eat with us tonight?"

She was washing her hands in the sink. "Okay, as long as you kids set the table."

Desmond sniffed the air and smiled. "That's a small price to pay for saving my stomach . . . and my life!"

Mom and I laughed.

As we grabbed the plates, Dad came into the kitchen from the basement.

"Is something wrong with the water heater?" Mom asked him. "The water isn't getting hot."

"Oh yeah," I said. "I had the same problem when I took my shower."

Let me tell you, cold showers aren't fun.

Dad nodded. "Yeah, it's acting up. I can fix it, but some of my tools are missing. They must be in one of the boxes we haven't unpacked."

Desmond and I looked at each other. We didn't say a word, but I knew we were both thinking the same thing: *Zax.*

Desmond changed the subject. "How was the bike park?"

"Good," I said, and I wanted to tell

him about it, but not in front of my
parents. The whole thing was too
weird. So instead I said, "You should
come next time. It's *scary* fun, if you
catch my drift."

Desmond's eyes lit up. "For real?"

I nodded, and we finished setting the table. Then I grabbed Desmond, and we went into the garage. I filled him in on the strange way my bike had acted at the track.

He inspected my bike closely. "Was it only *your* bike that went wild?"

"Nope," I told him. "Everyone's bike did."

Desmond's eyes sparked with excitement. "Let's check it out tomorrow," he said. "But first, let's eat. I'm starving!"

CHAPTER FIVE

KERSVILLE ELEMENTARY SCHOOL

The next day, I rode my bike to Kersville Elementary. Hmm, how do I describe this school?

For starters, a long, long time ago, it was a mansion where the founder of the town lived. Then it was a hospital. Finally, it became a school.

But it still didn't *feel* like a school. Some of the classrooms used to be bedrooms, and the cafeteria used to be the ballroom in the mansion.

It had round tables and creaky old chairs. Plus, it had huge chandeliers hanging from the ceiling. Who puts fancy crystal lights in a school?

The gym used to be the mansion's barn. You could still smell the horse stalls, which meant the gym smelled *pee-yew* gross.

The first time I saw the school, I was too scared to get out of the car. My parents had to practically carry me inside!

I don't think it's *totally scary* any-more, just a little creepy. There had to be ghosts in that building. But this story is about bikes . . . kind of.

Desmond was waiting for me at the bike rack. "Were any of these bikes at the park yesterday?"

Most of the bikes weren't the kind you'd ride at the track. Some had curved handlebars. Some had tassels and baskets. A few even had training wheels.

Finally, I noticed two from the track. One belonged to the girl who I saw wipe out. The other belonged to the boy who'd warned me about the Kicker.

"Those two bikes were at the park," I told Desmond.

Desmond pulled a weird camera from his backpack. I had never seen a camera like this one. It looked like a video-game controller. I watched as Desmond popped up the flash and took a picture of the two bikes. But the flash created a shadow on the bikes instead of making everything bright.

Desmond looked at the screen and whistled. "Totally ghostly."

He turned the camera around so I could see the screen. In the picture, the two bikes were covered in glowing dust.

"Does my bike look like that too?" I asked.

"Probably," Desmond said. "But you live with a ghost. Everything in your house looks like this in the right light."

He put the camera away, and we walked toward the school. "I'm sure about one thing," Desmond said. "Something is definitely haunting the racetrack."

CHAPTER SIX

GAME OVER, GHOST!

After school, Desmond and I went to the bike park. The Ghost Patrol needed to figure out what was going on at the track.

The girl and the boy were riding and practicing tricks. They weren't going near the Kicker.

I whispered to Desmond, "I hope they ride the track so you can see how haunted it is."

"The track might not be haunted," Desmond said. "Their *bikes* might be haunted. That's why we have to watch them, to see if the bikes do

strange things on their own." He nodded at the girl. "Like that!"

I looked over and saw the girl's bike hop into the air a few times. Both tires came off the ground at the same time. "She's doing a bunny hop," I told Desmond. "It's a bike trick."

"Hey! What about that?" Desmond asked. The boy was balancing on his front tire. The back tire was up in the air.

"That's called a stoppie," I said.

"It's another trick. Wow, you really don't ride bikes, do you?"

Desmond shrugged. "I do not."

"Well, I ride bikes, and those bikes aren't haunted," I said.

After an hour of watching the boy and girl, Desmond couldn't take it anymore. He yelled, "Hey, how come you two aren't riding the Kicker today?"

"Ask your friend," the boy replied, pointing to me. "He fell so hard yesterday that no one else wants to ride it."

My face flushed hot. It was not cool being the kid *everybody* saw wipe out.

So in a flash, I hopped on my bike and put on

my helmet. There was only one way to prove the Kicker was haunted. I needed to ride the track again. But I had a plan this time.

I went to the top of the track and pedaled down the hill as fast as I could. I picked up speed with each turn and each jump.

"Go, Andres!" Desmond screamed. Everyone at the bike park clapped and cheered too.

Then, right before I reached the Kicker, I put my plan into action. I jumped off my bike.

As I crash-landed in the mud, all those cheers stopped.

My bike, on the other hand, kept going.

It jumped the Kicker, flew into a front flip, then landed perfectly and skidded to a stop. It was the craziest, coolest, creepiest thing ever! If I hadn't seen it with my own eyes, I wouldn't have believed it.

Thankfully, Desmond was right there. He knew what to do.

Desmond snapped a picture of my bike with his special camera. "Game over, ghost!" he announced. He ran over and showed me the screen.

What I saw made my heart do a front flip in my chest.

There was a ghost sitting on my bike, smiling from one ghostly ear to the other. And why wouldn't he be happy?

That ghost just landed the Kicker.

CHAPTER SEVEN

GHOST TRICKS

Slowly, the ghost appeared in real life. Everyone gasped. I gasped too, because that's what normal people do when they see a ghost.

"Did you see that trick?" the ghost asked excitedly and floated over to us. "It was awesome!"

I stood up from the mud. "Yeah, but you can't kick kids off bikes like that."

"It's not cool," added Desmond. "Not cool at all."

The ghost looked from Desmond
to me to the other kids, who stood
with their eyes wide open. Then he
stopped smiling.

"Oh, I am so sorry," the ghost said.
"I didn't mean to bother anyone.
I just love this track. I've been fly-
ing around here for a long time, but
I could never jump the Kicker. I'm
a ghost, so I just pass right through
the ramp every time."

I remembered Zax trying to pass through the wall with the ratchet. "You needed a real bike to jump the ramp."

The ghost nodded. "I only wanted to borrow one for a second."

"Maybe you could have asked first," I suggested.

"Yeah, I tried that once and scared a kid pretty bad," admitted the ghost. "But thanks to you, I finally landed the jump!"

"And you nailed it!" I cheered and high-fived the ghost.

"I know, right?" The ghost beamed.

Desmond was really excited. I could tell because he always asked questions when he was excited.  "How did you hold on to a moving bike? If you go up, do you have to come back down? Is riding a bike as a ghost easier than riding a bike as a not-ghost?"

"Those are ghost secrets, my friend," the ghost replied.

Now I'm positive that I don't like ghost secrets.

The ghost grabbed my bike and floated it back to me. "Here. Thank

you for helping my dream come true."

I took the handlebars and nodded to the ghost. "Hey, do you have a name?"

"You can call me Kicker," he said. Then Kicker faded away.

Desmond patted me on the back. "Congratulations, Andres. You just solved your first case!"

Now *I* was the one smiling. I have to admit, it felt great.

Back in my garage, Desmond studied my bike. I was wiping mud off my arms with a towel because there was no way I was going to take another cold shower. I'd rather be muddy *and* stinky.

Zax floated in looking for the tool-box again. He grabbed a wrench.

"Are you ever going to tell me what you're up to, Zax?" I asked.

"It's a surprise," he said. Then he floated back inside through the open door.

Desmond and I glanced at each other. We knew what we had to do.

We followed Zax and pressed up against the wall like spies. He went down to the basement and floated to the water heater. Desmond and I hid behind him on the dark stairs and watched.

Zax used the wrench to unscrew something.

Suddenly, I felt the icy chill of the truth. Zax definitely broke the water heater!

Before I could do anything, Zax said, "You guys can come out now. You're not very good at hiding."

Desmond and I stood up slowly.

"Did you break our water heater?" I asked. "I have been taking cold showers, you know!"

Zax put down the wrench. "I didn't break the water heater. I just fixed it."

"Fixed it?" I said. Then I turned to Desmond and asked, "Do ghosts fix stuff?"

Desmond shrugged like he had no idea.

Zax nodded. "Ghosts love to fix stuff. People hear clanging sounds and think we're haunting places, but that's just us fixing things. I love when everything runs smoothly."

"Wow," said Desmond. "I did not know that."

I couldn't believe it. Something Desmond Cole didn't know about ghosts? Now I'd heard it all.

"I need to go
write this down
in my ghost note-
book," said Desmond
as he took off up the
stairs. "Thanks, Zax! And,
Andres, please go take a
shower. I didn't want to say
anything, but you kinda smell."

"Oh yeah, ghosts can smell, too," admitted Zax as he held his nose. "Can you please go take a *long* shower?"

I laughed because he didn't have to tell me twice.

CHAPTER EIGHT

A NEW CASE

The next day after school, Desmond and I were still talking about Zax.

"Ghosts still surprise me," said Desmond. "They're always up to something new."

That was when a few of the kids from the bike park ran up to me. It was the first time I had seen them without their bikes.

"Andres!" exclaimed one of the girls. "You have to help us!"

"Yeah," another kid said. "Our bikes have been stolen. We think that ghost did it."

Desmond stepped in. "Hold on, everybody. Ghosts don't steal. At least, I don't think they steal."

I wasn't so sure. "This could be another ghost secret," I whispered to Desmond. "What if Kicker really wanted to steal all our bikes?"

That's when we heard the screams.

We ran over to the bike rack, where more kids were yelling. Only, the rack was practically empty, and most of the bikes were now riding away *on their own*!

They looked like runaway shopping carts rolling down the street. And *my* bike was there too!

Desmond and I took off chasing after the bikes, but they were fast.

"It's no use," said Desmond, who was breathing hard from running. "We'll never catch them on foot."

He ran back and found a little girl with a purple bike. It had handlebars with pink and purple tassels.

"Can I please borrow your bike and your helmet?" Desmond asked.

"Sure," the girl said.

Desmond hopped on the little bike. And that's when things got really weird!

CHAPTER NINE

DESMOND'S DARING RUN

As the bikes rode down the hill, Desmond chased after them. He pedaled so fast that the little bike wobbled from side to side.

I figured one thing out right away: Desmond Cole did not know how to ride a bike.

It was a good thing he had training wheels!

As he picked up speed, the pink and purple tassels blew in the breeze. I tried to run after him, but he was too fast.

I lost him after they reached the forest. It seemed like the stolen bikes were heading straight for the bike park on the other side.

What happened next? I couldn't
tell you because I wasn't there.

But Desmond was. And this is
what he told me:

Chasing after those bikes was the

scariest thing he'd ever done.

"STOP! PLEASE! STOP!" he yelled, holding on to the bike for dear life. He was going so fast that the training wheels started to smoke!

The bikes ahead of him turned onto a trail that led straight to the bike park. Desmond watched as the stolen bikes swerved and hopped over a fallen branch.

Then he remembered the bunny hop trick, so he tried it.

And it worked! That tiny bike made it over the branch! Desmond turned and followed the bikes, which were already at the start of the track.

By now, one thing was clear to Desmond. He was going to have to ride the racetrack!

He held his breath as
he drove down the first hill.
Clouds of dirt kicked up from
the bikes. Desmond was covered
in dust. He must have looked
ridiculous, riding the track on a bike
with training wheels and tassels!

But if you were the only kid in town

who knew how to investigate ghosts, then you probably got used to doing ridiculous things.

As he raced around the track, every bike in front of him fell over, one after another. Even with all the crashing, he kept his focus on the first stolen bike.

Which was my bike!

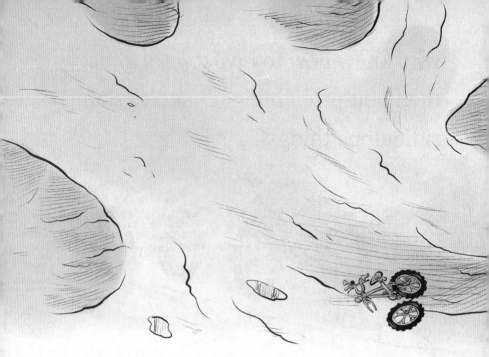

Desmond had almost reached my bike when it crashed. He tried to stop, but it was too late. Desmond was going up the Kicker.

His wheels blazed like a mini-rocket launched into orbit! The tassels on the handlebars fluttered like

tiny hands reaching for help. And
Desmond . . . well, Desmond was
screaming his head off.

There was no way Desmond could
land the Kicker.

Desmond held on to the bike and prepared to hit the ground hard. But something froze him in midair. Desmond hovered above the ramp, and then he floated safely to the ground.

I might not have believed that part if I hadn't seen it with my own eyes.

When the other kids made it to the park, they started screaming. All their bikes were scattered on the track, totally destroyed. Mine, too. Broken frames, busted wheels—the place looked like a bike graveyard.

Then Kicker the ghost appeared. He had saved Desmond.

"I was hoping you would catch me," Desmond told Kicker.

"Happy to help," Kicker said.

I ran down to join them. "Kicker, did you steal our bikes?"

"It wasn't Kicker," said Desmond. "Will the real ghost thief please appear?"

With a bright shimmer, another ghost formed in front of us.

"Who are *you*?" Desmond asked.

"I'm Hal," he said. "I took your bikes."

All the kids started booing him.

"I was going to give them back," Hal said. "I only took the bikes that needed a tune-up."

Oh boy, I thought. *Another ghost who likes to fix things!*

Desmond quieted the crowd to let Hal explain himself.

The ghost took off his hat and put it over where his ghost heart might be. "You kids were riding on bikes with tires that need air, chains that are too tight, and handlebars that are too loose. It was driving me crazy! I had to do something to make it better."

Someone in the crowd yelled, "So what are we going to do now? All our bikes are ruined!"

Desmond and I looked at each other, because we had an idea that everyone would love.

CHAPTER TEN

Hal the Bike Healer

Here's a secret: Not all ghost secrets are bad.

I mean, take Hal for example. All he wants to do is fix broken bikes. Now that's exactly what he does! He fixed every single bike that day, even mine.

He does good work, too. In fact, he got rid of my dents and repainted the frame. I don't even need that electrical tape on the seat anymore. My bike is like new.

Hal is such a good mechanic that Desmond and I helped him set up his own repair shop at the bike park. He

gives free tune-ups, and he's right there to fix our bikes whenever we crash.

Oh, and as for Kicker, it turns out he's a great bike-riding instructor. Right now, he's working with one of his most challenging students ever: Desmond Cole.

At least whenever Desmond falls, Kicker is right there for him.

Maybe this Ghost Patrol thing is like riding a bike: Once you learn how to do it, you never forget.